Always be a
Cardinal
fan !

"

Jack Boyd

For my father,
the greatest storyteller ever.

For my mother,
for sharing her love of baseball.

For my husband,
for supporting me.

For Jack, Daniel, and Molly,
this book is for you.

- Jackie Polys

PRT0115B

Printed in the United States

ISBN-13: 9781620863732
ISBN-10: 1620863731

www.mascotbooks.com

RALSTON

THE RALLY SQUIRREL

JACKIE POLYS

ILLUSTRATED BY
TAYLOR FRESHLEY

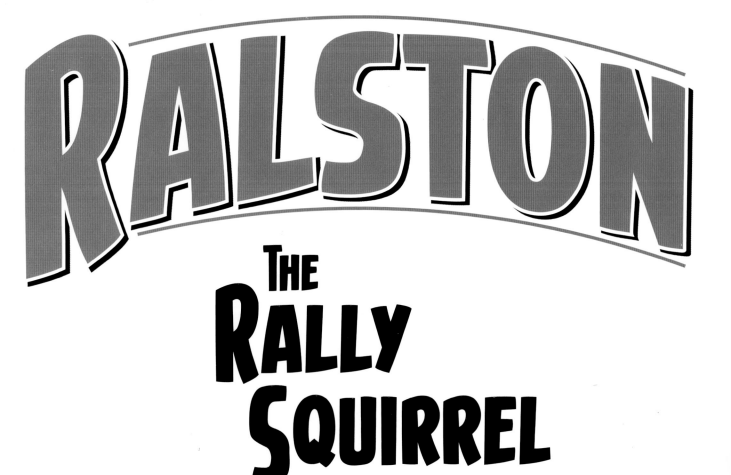

Ralston was excited! In just one week it would be his birthday and opening day of the Birds' season. He could hardly contain his excitement. His tail couldn't stop twitching and all he could talk about was getting opening day tickets for his birthday.

Rally (as his friends called him) was like most squirrels his age. He spent his days dreaming of baseball season and someday going to watch a game at the stadium.

There was one problem: his dad. Nothing made Dad grumpier than talk of baseball and taxes. "Who wants to pay money to

watch them lose?" he would ask. "Do you know how much those tickets cost?" Rally knew what his father would say. He had been saying it for years. But it never stopped Rally from asking.

Rally spent his afternoons staring at the baseball posters in his room in the tiny tree they called home. They couldn't live near the stadium like everyone else because his dad said it cost too much...something about taxes being too high. Rally wasn't sure what taxes were (they hadn't covered that in third grade yet), but he knew it meant they would never live near the stadium.

Rally was embarrassed to tell people they lived under the checkerboard sign. And he hated sharing a room with his little brother, Archie, while his sister, Nestle, got her own room. But they were lucky enough to live next to an apartment building and that meant they could listen to Birds' games through open windows.

Rally liked listening to the games with his brother anyway. It wasn't fun watching the game with Dad. The moment the team showed signs of weakness, Dad would head home, tail erect, screaming all the way, even if the Birds were winning! So embarrassing.

Luckily, Mom was an ally. Sometimes she would sneak away with the boys to watch the game in peace. She even brought popcorn and peanut crumbs for them to snack on while they watched. Pretty cool...for a mom, anyway.

Every year since he could remember, Rally asked for tickets to opening day for his birthday. He imagined what it would be like to watch his hometown heroes play from the best seats in the house: under the dugout bench. He would have one cheek full of hot dog crumbs and the other full of pretzels. He would hear the crack of the bat and feel the dust against his fur. He would smell the fear of the other team...

Every year Rally had asked...and every year he was disappointed.

There was always a reason Dad wouldn't pay for tickets. "We have to make drey payments, pay taxes, and buy you nuts, Rally. Do you know how much it costs to feed you?" his dad would ask. "If you stop eating and get a job, you can go to a game."

Funny, thought Rally. *Real funny, Dad.*

Finally, his birthday arrived. After stuffing as much pizza and cake as possible in his cheeks without making Mom mad, it was time to open presents. One by one, Rally would open a gift and toss it aside—barely thanking anyone. *Come on*, he thought, *it's got to be here somewhere!* But as Rally looked around, he didn't see any presents that looked like tickets. His tail went flat.

With a sly grin, Uncle Auggie presented Rally with his final gift. Rally just knew opening day tickets would be in that envelope!

And that's when he saw it. The date on the two tickets he held in his paws. It wasn't for a game in April…it was for a game in October?

What in the world was this? Rally didn't want postseason tickets he was probably never going to use! He wanted opening day tickets! *Crazy optimists*, he thought. Rally was heartbroken.

Archie always tried to look on the bright side. "Don't worry," said Archie. "This will be the Birds' season! We'll get to that game in October."

What? Did Rally hear him correctly? Did Archie expect to go to the game with him? But Archie was right. Because Archie's birthday was right after Rally's, it was a joint gift. *Well, isn't this the icing on my day*, Rally thought. It had become the worst birthday ever.

Opening day came with Rally watching the game through the pawn shop window. The Birds weren't doing well this season. June and July were just as disastrous. Rally put his tickets away, knowing he wouldn't need them.

Of all seasons, why this year? Why couldn't they just win? Of course, how could they win when so many of their star players were on the DL? Rally couldn't even pronounce half the names on the batting list.

August came and went with the Birds racking up more losses. Rally focused on swimming, chasing birds, and throwing acorns at people, (even though Mom told him to stop). However, none of this distracted from the Birds' losses.

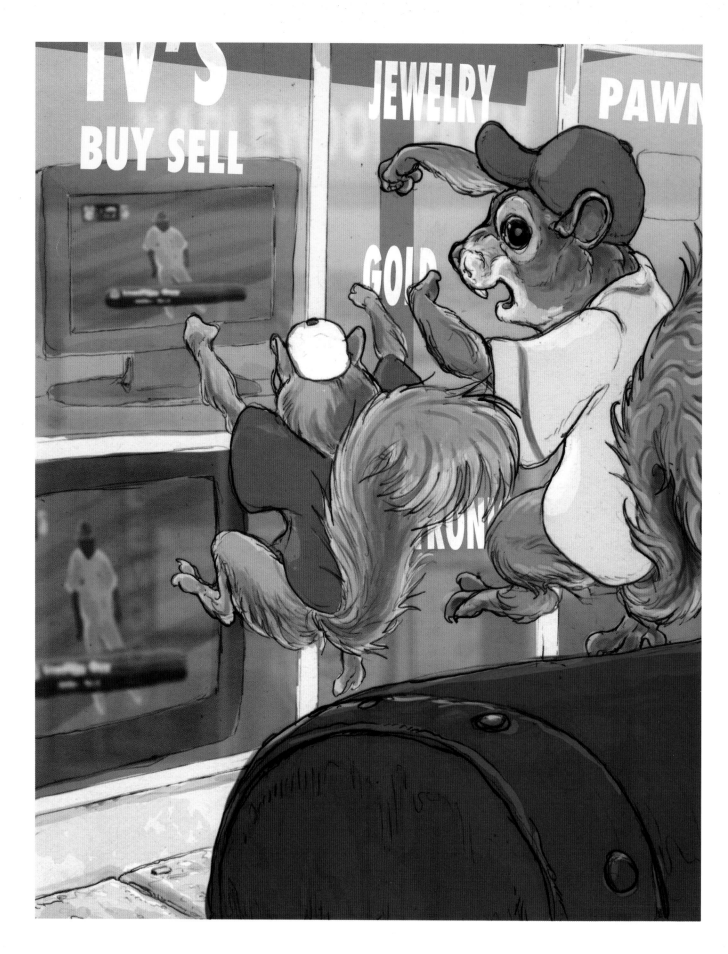

September arrived with cooler weather, trees changing color, and acorns aplenty. And wouldn't you know, Rally's hometown heroes were starting to win games. Rally paid close attention in math that year so he could figure out the Birds' chances of making playoffs. Even with their wins, the chances were only 8-percent. But by mid-September, it rose to 18-percent...and just a week later, they were up to almost 25-percent.

Dad made sure he didn't get too excited. After every win, he would remind Rally that those wins didn't mean much. Too much had to go right and everyone knew they would flop. He sure knew how to get Rally's tail in a knot!

But Dad was wrong! It became the greatest late-season comeback in the history of baseball! The Birds defeated the odds. Everything had fallen into place, and they crushed the other team in a final blow that earned them wild card entry into the National League Championships!

R ally started to panic. Where had he put those tickets? What game were they for? He prayed his crazy optimist aunt and uncle had gotten him tickets for game one or two of the playoffs. If it were game five or six, Rally may never see a game.

Just before he was going to hunt Archie down and accuse him of taking the tickets, Rally saw them sticking out from under his bed of twigs. Quickly, he scanned the ticket for the date. Yes! Game three of the playoffs! Rally gave out a "Woo-hoo!" and flipped his tail. He and Archie were going to a game at last!

Rally's tail could not stop twitching the day of the big game. Every five seconds, he would ask his parents if it was time to go. Meanwhile, Dad was patiently trying to tell Rally all the things he would need to know once they got to the stadium—like how to get to their seats, how to get to the bathroom, and what to do if they got separated. In all of his excitement, Rally only heard a little bit of the instructions.

The moment they entered the stadium, Rally was in Heaven. It was everything he knew it would be. His team had the best fans in baseball.

Rally found their seats easily. Down some steps, behind the smelly locker room, through a long tunnel, and out they popped onto a ledge under the dugout roof. They could see everything! Rally found some popcorn for himself and peanut shells for Archie and they settled in to watch the game.

Rally was so into the game, he hadn't noticed Archie fidgeting. When Rally finally looked over, Archie had a panicked look on his face. *Aww man*, thought Rally, *Archie has to go pee. Why can't he control himself like a normal squirrel?*

Rally reluctantly set off to find a bathroom with Archie. Rally wished he had listened to Dad's instructions. He couldn't have Archie running home and saying he hadn't listened, so he needed to find a bathroom, and fast. There was a tunnel that led to the back of the stadium, and he thought Dad said the bathrooms were there.

At the end of the tunnel, there was a hole that looked like it led to the bathroom. Rally told Archie to sit tight while he investigated. But as Rally went through the hole, he immediately realized the massive mistake he made. This was no bathroom! This was the outfield!

How had this happened? Rally was frantic as he tried to race back to the hole he had come out of, but he didn't know where it had gone. There were players yelling and running at him, and the crowd growing louder. He knew he needed to get out of there.

He finally found the hole, grabbed Archie, and they raced into the next hole. Thankfully, that hole led to the bathroom. He got Archie there just in time. Man, he was a pain of a brother.

Archie wanted to know everything as soon as they were back in their seats. "Wally," (his brother couldn't say the "r" sound) "what did you do? What happened out there? Where did that hole lead to?"

"Don't you worry about that," Rally snarled. "It was nothing." Rally was humiliated. He couldn't believe he ended up on the field. He was just glad Archie wasn't with him so he couldn't run home and tell on him. He knew if Dad found out, this would be the last game for him...forever.

That's when Rally saw something that made his heart stop. Archie saw it too. The two brothers just sat there, tails erect, eyes wide.

Rally was on the jumbotron.

Rally stared. Archie stared. This could not be happening. Rally had only been out there for a second! How had he managed to get himself on TV? As his mind raced, an even more terrifying thought began to enter his mind.

"You know Dad is watching the game, wight?" Archie asked in a whisper.

Rally saw his life flash before his eyes. He tried to think of some way out of this. Some way of explaining what he'd done. But facts are facts. Rally hadn't listened to Dad's instructions and gotten lost. He would be punished for this.

Rally couldn't enjoy the rest of the game. Instead he focused on how to get out of the mess he was in.

Rally and Archie walked home as slowly as possible. Maybe Rally would have time to think of some way out of this. Amazingly, his brother was being very cool. He stayed quiet and left Rally alone.

As they approached the house, Rally was surprised not to hear Dad yelling. Maybe he was so mad he couldn't even speak.

Reluctantly, Rally entered the drey. As he walked in the door, he knew he was in for it. This wasn't like when he made fart jokes or pretended he was peeing on stuff. Nope. This was a major league mess up. He was on the field! He had interrupted major league play!

But when he looked up, there was Dad sitting in his favorite spot waiting for his dinner. And even better, he had a big smile on his face.

"**W**ell, look who it is! Our hero for the day!" Dad yelled.

Rally was confused. Why wasn't Dad screaming at him? Wait. Did he say hero?

"Rally," Dad continued, "you are a hero. Didn't you see yourself on TV?"

Rally thought for a minute. Sure, he saw himself on the jumbotron, but he must have been so busy thinking about the mess he was in that he missed something very important.

Dad went on, "The Birds won the game and all because of you! Afterwards, they decided to adopt you as their unofficial mascot!"

Rally felt like he was dreaming. He couldn't believe it!

The phone didn't stop ringing all night. Everyone Rally knew was calling. They wanted to know everything about the game. How had he gotten on the field? What gave him the idea to go on the field? Rally wasn't going to admit it was all a terrible mistake now that he was a hero. He threatened Archie to keep it under wraps if he knew what was good for him.

The best phone call was from Uncle Auggie. He'd decided Rally needed to attend the next game.

The next day Rally woke, showered, dressed, ate, and brushed his teeth in record speed. Then he waited. And waited. Then he bothered Mom. Then he bothered Archie. Then he bothered Nestle. His mom was just about to sell him to the circus when Uncle Auggie picked him up and they were finally off to Game 4.

Rally was excited to be at the game with his favorite uncle. And he was feeling pretty proud of himself as well. Who wouldn't when everywhere he looked he saw fans holding squirrel signs, little kids holding stuffed animal squirrels, and shirts with squirrels on them? *People are odd,* thought Rally. He was pretty happy he was a squirrel.

The Birds had a nice 3-2 lead, but Rally wished it were bigger. With just a one-run lead anything could happen. His uncle must have been thinking the same thing because he leaned over and said, "Rally, I think they need your help."

Holy wow! thought Rally. *He wants me to go on the field again! I can't do that! Last night was a mistake.* How was he going to get out of this?

Rally realized there was no way around it. He was going to have to show everyone what he was made of.

Rally looked up, and Uncle Auggie gave him a nudge. He took a deep breath and scampered toward the opening of the dugout. He could see the batter clearly. Without another thought, Rally ran as fast as he could across home plate. Right through the batter's legs!

Rally's little stunt caused enough commotion to help the Birds win the game once again. And Rally had forever secured his status as a hometown hero and unofficial mascot.

But best of all...he knew he would never have to beg for tickets ever again.

Jackie Polys grew up listening to Cardinal games on the radio as a child. While her mother instilled a love for the game of baseball, her father taught her how to tell stories. After years of enjoying baseball and storytelling, she is thrilled to have combined the two to bring Ralston the Rally Squirrel *to children everywhere.*